Barney Bipple's Magic Dandelions

Barney Bipple's Magic Dandelions

by Carol Chapman · pictures by Steven Kellogg

E. P. DUTTON · NEW YORK

Text copyright © 1977 by Carol Chapman
Illustrations copyright © 1977, 1988 by Steven Kellogg

Library of Congress Cataloging in Publication Data
Chapman, Carol A.   Barney Bipple's magic dandelions.
   SUMMARY: Barney Bipple doesn't heed Miss Merkle's
suggestion concerning complicated wishes until it is
almost too late.
   [1. Wishes—Fiction]   I. Kellogg, Steven.   II. Title.
PZ7.C36636Bar   [E]   77-5747   ISBN: 0-525-44449-1

Published in the United States by E. P. Dutton,
2 Park Avenue, New York, N.Y. 10016,
a division of NAL Penguin Inc.

Published simultaneously in Canada by
Fitzhenry & Whiteside Limited, Toronto

Editor: Ann Durell

Printed in Hong Kong by South China Printing Co.
Revised Edition   10 9 8 7 6 5 4 3 2 1

loving bouquets of magic dandelions

to all my family and friends
C.C.
to Phil, Alma, Vanessa, Derek, Brian and Jennifer
S.K.

Barney Bipple was six. But he wanted to be eight. He wanted to be eight so he could play with Hector and Gerald.

He also wanted a big, shiny car like his Uncle Jason had. Everyone called him Jace the Ace 'cause his car was so neat.

And he wanted his dog, Snoozer, to talk. Barney was sure that dogs had a lot of interesting things to talk about.

Now, it just so happened that next door to Barney Bipple lived an old woman named Minerva Merkle. Everyone thought she was rich because she had a lot of jewels and furs.

One day, Barney saw a huge diamond on Miss Merkle's lawn. He knocked at her door and handed it to her politely. "Such a nice boy," said Miss Merkle. "I think I will give you a reward."

She took him into her backyard. It was covered with white, puffy dandelions. Miss Merkle picked three and handed them to Barney.

"Make a wish, blow on a dandelion, and your wish will come true. But stick to simple wishes, like for diamonds and furs. If you need more, just let me know."

Barney thanked Miss Merkle and went home. Not wanting furs or diamonds, he wished he was eight, then blew the puff. And in an instant, the snap on his pants popped, his shoes became tight, and he was eight.

He ran down to Hector's house. "Can you play?"
asked Barney in his new, older voice.
"Sure," said Hector. "You must be a new kid."
"Sort of," said Barney.

And Barney and Hector found Gerald, and they all played baseball.

After Hector and Gerald went home, Barney made his second wish. His dog, Snoozer, looked up at him and said, "Do you know I cannot stand my dry dog food? There are many different brands, but the kind your mother buys is the worst!" "Wouldn't you like to tell me about some adventures?" asked Barney.

"What adventures? All I do is eat and sleep. I did have an interesting dream about a steak once," said Snoozer. "Forget it," said Barney. "I guess it's time to make my third wish." This time he wished extra hard, then blew on his last puff.

And zap! He was sitting in a long, shiny, yellow car.
And the engine was roaring.
Barney stepped on the gas. And off he went, racing down
the street, around the block, and onto the freeway.

"Neat!" said Barney, going a hundred miles an hour.
Pretty soon he heard a siren.
"Oh, *oh*," he said.

When he finally found the brake pedal, he stopped the car.
"Okay," said the officer. "Let me see your license."
"I don't have one," said Barney.
"What about the registration for the car?" asked the officer.
"I don't know what that is," said Barney.

The officer took off his sunglasses. "Hey, you're just a kid!" he exclaimed.
So the officer drove Barney down to the police station and called Barney's mother.

"Mom!" cried Barney when he saw her.
"There must be some mistake," said Mrs. Bipple. "My son is six and this boy is eight." And she left.

"Looks like you're in a lot of trouble," said the officer. "Driving a stolen car and saying you're someone's kid when you're not."

Barney felt very sad. Then suddenly he had an idea.
"Can I make a phone call?" he asked.
"Sure," said the officer.

Five minutes later Minerva Merkle arrived carrying a
dandelion. She gave it to Barney.
"See what happens when your wishes are complicated?"
said Miss Merkle.
Barney nodded and closed his eyes tight. "I wish away
all those other wishes," he said.

In an instant he was in his own front yard. Snoozer barked, Gerald and Hector walked by ignoring him, and Barney knew he'd never see that yellow car again.

Barney ran into his house.

"Do you know who I am?" he asked his mom.

"You're Barney Bipple, my six-year-old boy,"
said Mrs. Bipple.

"Right!" yelled Barney, giving his mother a giant hug.

And he never made complicated wishes again.

Just simple wishes, like for a bike,

a steak for Snoozer,   a radio,

a baby brother,

a new mitt,

a frog,   gum,

a pony… and stuff like that.

CAROL CHAPMAN says, "The seed for this book was planted when I first blew upon a dandelion and made a wish. It was reinforced years later when I taught my daughter this age-old superstition."

Ms. Chapman lives in Burbank, California.

STEVEN KELLOGG had great fun illustrating this book. He could identify with Barney, because as a child he often fantasized about being bigger and older. Miss Merkle is patterned after his grandmother, "who had a gift for sharing things with a child and making them seem magic and wonderful." Jace the Ace is patterned after his brother-in-law, a Grand Prix International driving champion.